ISBN 1 85854 526 9
© Brimax Books Ltd 1996. All rights reserved.
Published by Brimax Books Ltd, Newmarket, England CB8 7AU 1996.
Printed in France - n° 68741

Stories You Can Read

by Lucy Kincaid
Illustrated by Eric Kincaid

Brimax · Newmarket · England

Presents for Pipkin

Pipkin Rabbit is staying with his Grandma and Grandpa. They live in Long Grass Lane.

Grandpa is digging the potato patch.
Pipkin is helping.

Grandpa is hot. He takes off his hat.
"I can hold it for you, Grandpa," says Pipkin.

Pipkin puts the hat on. It is too big.
He can see his toes but that is all.

Now Pipkin tries to dig with Grandpa's shovel. It is too heavy. He falls over.

Grandma and Grandpa have a surprise.
They give Pipkin two packages.

There is a hat inside one package.
There is a shovel inside the other package.

"Grandpa looks like a big Pipkin and Pipkin looks like a little Grandpa," laughs Grandma.

"Where shall I dig?" asks Pipkin.
"You can clear the weeds from Grandma's
flower bed," says Grandpa.

Grandpa is busy. He does not watch what Pipkin is doing. Pipkin is busy too.

Weeds and flowers look the same to Pipkin.
He digs them all up.

"Oh dear!" says Grandpa, when he sees what Pipkin has done.

"I was trying to help," sobs Pipkin.
"I know," says Grandpa, drying Pipkin's tears.

Grandpa sorts out the flowers and the weeds.
He puts the flowers back where they belong.

The flower bed is full of flowers again but it is full of footprints too.

"We must clear those footprints away," says Grandpa. Grandpa lets Pipkin do it.

All the footprints are gone. Pipkin sees
Grandma coming. He hides in the long grass.

Grandpa tells Grandma what has happened. "Oh dear!" says Grandma. She calls Pipkin.

"I am sorry, Grandma," says Pipkin.
"Please let me keep my shovel."

"Of course you can," says Grandma.
Pipkin is happy now. He gives Grandma
a big kiss.

A Windy Day

It is a windy day. Grandma is washing sheets.
Pipkin is helping her.

"The wind will soon blow the sheets dry,"
says Grandma.

Grandma is waiting for the next peg.
"Can you go a little faster?" she asks.

Grandma is called away. There are still two sheets left to hang up. Pipkin has an idea.

Pipkin asks Grandpa to help.
"This is not as easy as it looks," says Grandpa.

The wind is playing tricks. It is pulling at the pegs. The pegs are getting loose.

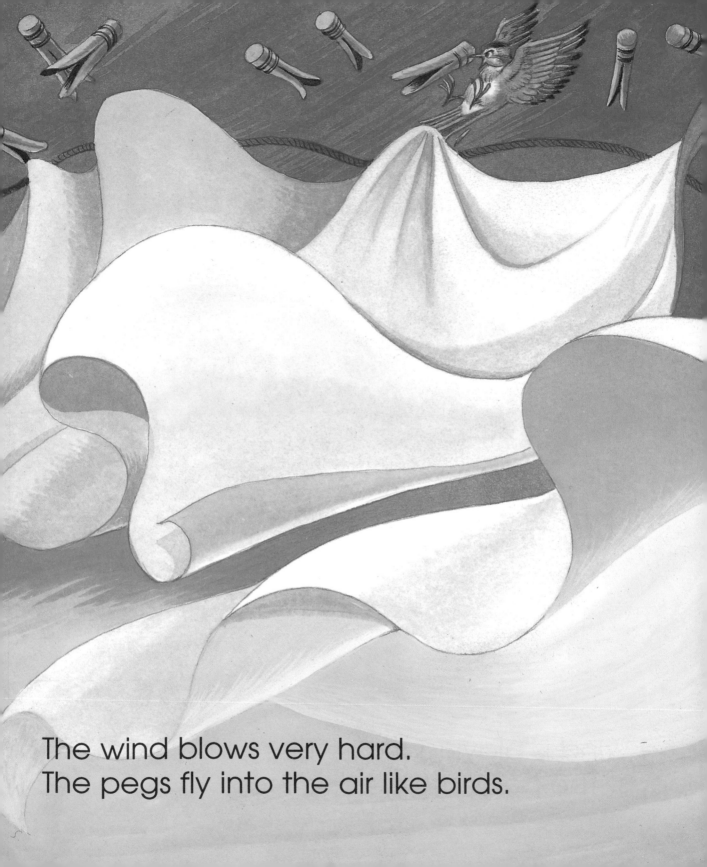

The wind blows very hard.
The pegs fly into the air like birds.

Pipkin can see what is going to happen.
"Look out, Grandpa!" he shouts. He is too late.

Before Grandpa can move, a flying sheet
wraps itself around him.
"Help!" shouts Grandpa.

The more Pipkin tries to untangle Grandpa,
the more tangled Grandpa gets.

Grandma screams. She thinks Pipkin
is fighting with a ghost.

"Don't be afraid," says Pipkin. "It's only
Grandpa."
"Get me out of here!" shouts Grandpa.

Grandma takes charge.
"Keep still," she says to Grandpa.
"Unwind that way," she says to Pipkin.

"Are you all right?" asks Pipkin.
"I think so," says Grandpa.
Grandma takes the sheet to wash it again.

"Look up there!" gasps Pipkin.
"What shall we do, Grandpa?"

Grandma will be cross if she sees the sheet on the roof. They must do something quickly.

"Hurry up!" whispers Pipkin.
"I am hurrying!" whispers Grandpa.
Grandpa has hidden the sheet.

Grandpa makes sure the sheet will not blow away again. He pushes the pegs down very hard.

The wind cannot pull the pegs off.
Grandma cannot pull the pegs off either.
Pipkin goes to get Grandpa.

"How did your sweater get like that?"
asks Grandma. Grandpa and Pipkin know,
but they are not telling.

The Tunnel

Pipkin and Grandma are picking berries.
Grandma knows where the best berries grow.

It is very quiet. The only sound is the buzzing of the bees.

Suddenly there is another sound.
"I can hear someone crying," says Pipkin.

"Unhook me please," says Grandma.
"Look over there," says Pipkin.

"We have just come across the road," says Mother Rabbit. "And Bobby has got left behind."

Poor Bobby. He is too little and too frightened to cross the road by himself.

Mother Rabbit cannot leave her babies by themselves. She does not know what to do.

"Leave this to me," says Grandma.
"Shout if you see anything coming, Pipkin."

Pipkin is glad Grandma and Bobby are safe.
Everyone else is pleased too.

Pipkin tells Grandpa how brave Grandma
was. Grandpa looks very thoughtful.

Pipkin and Grandpa are busy.
"That looks like a good idea," says Grandma.

"Can we start digging now?" says Pipkin.
"The sooner the better," says Grandpa.

Everyone stops to ask what Grandpa and
Pipkin are doing.
"Look at the plan," says Grandpa.

Everyone wants to help. Everyone goes
home to get something to dig with.

The hole is getting deeper. It is changing into a tunnel. Where is it going?

The tunnel gets longer and darker. Grandpa
hangs up a lantern to give some light.

Digging is hard work. Everyone gets thirsty.
Grandma comes with drinks on a tray.

Finally the tunnel is finished.
"Hello Grandma!" shouts Pipkin.

Now everyone can go under the road instead of over the road.

Now even the smallest rabbit is safe.

Apples for Sale

The apples on the apple tree are ripe.
It is time to pick them.

"I will hold the ladder steady," says Pipkin.

Grandpa is going to sell some apples.
First he must put up a stall.

Grandpa takes the apples out of the barrel.
Pipkin puts a shine on the apples.

"Grandma is calling me," says Grandpa.
"I will look after the stall," says Pipkin.

"Apples for sale!" shouts Pipkin.
He hopes someone comes along soon.

Everyone comes to buy apples.
Pipkin is very busy.

Grandpa is gone a long time.
Pipkin sells all the apples.

Little Tom has run a long way.
"Can I buy one of your apples?" he asks.

"Is there one left in the barrel?" asks Tom.
"I will look," says Pipkin.

Pipkin stands on his tiptoes. He can see an apple. He cannot quite reach it.

"I have it!" shouts Pipkin. And then
he falls head first into the barrel.

The barrel wobbles. It falls over.
It begins to roll. Pipkin is still inside it.

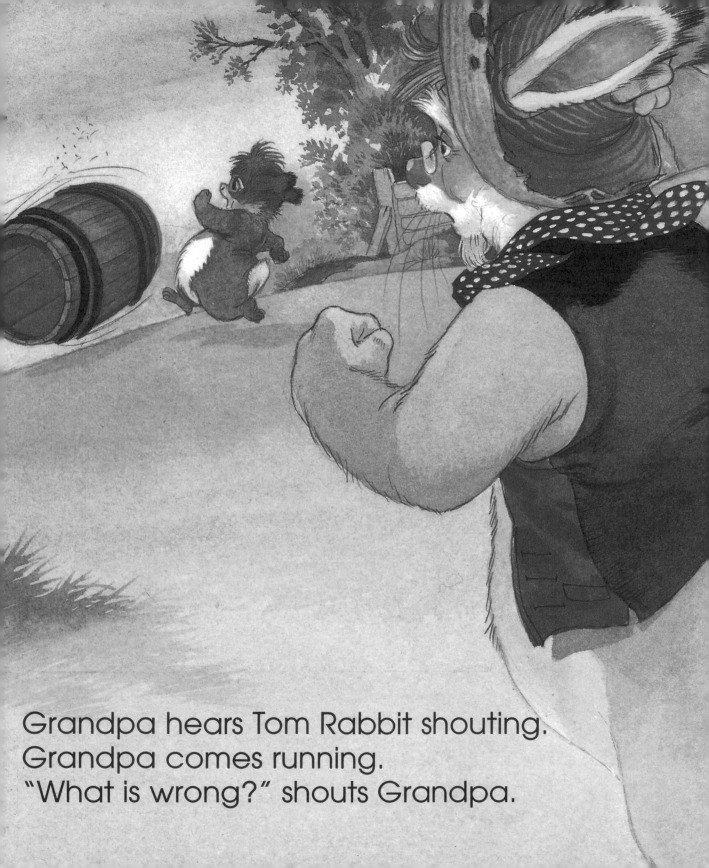

Grandpa hears Tom Rabbit shouting.
Grandpa comes running.
"What is wrong?" shouts Grandpa.

"Stop! Stop!" shouts Grandpa.
"Stop! Stop!" shouts Tom Rabbit.

"I would if I could!" shouts Pipkin from
inside the barrel.

"Where am I going?" shouts Pipkin as he flies into the air.

"Into the pond!" shouts Grandpa.
What a big splash Pipkin makes!

Pipkin is wet and very dizzy.
But what is he holding?

"This is the best apple I have ever tasted,"
says Tom.
"Well done Pipkin!" says Grandpa.